THE SECRET TUNNEL

They worked at their end of the secret passage

THE SECRET TUNNEL

ELISABETH BATT

Illustrated by
Lorna Paull

LUTTERWORTH PRESS · LONDON

First published 1970
Copyright © 1970 by Lutterworth Press

ISBN 0 7188 1621 8

*Printed in Great Britain by Richard Clay (The Chaucer Press), Ltd.,
Bungay, Suffolk*

CONTENTS

Paul Hears the News

THE boys and girls at Holly School didn't need to look at the clock on the classroom wall to know that it was time to go home. Everybody in that part of the town knew that it was a quarter to four because of the noise made by the children coming out of Castle Street primary school. Mrs. Lester, who taught at Holly School, paid no attention to the confused roar in the next street; she signed to her pupils to put their pencils and books away tidily and to leave the room quietly, the boys standing aside to let the girls go first. "It's never too early to learn good manners," she often told them.

She stood at the door and said good-bye to each one as they filed past her, and each in turn said, "Good-bye, Mrs. Lester."

She smiled very kindly at Paul Harvey who was one of the last to leave. All her pupils were well-behaved, clean, tidy, and well-dressed, but Paul was her favourite. He was so quick and eager to learn, attentive in class, interested in all that she taught him. It had not been necessary to teach him good manners; it was natural to him to behave well.

Paul hesitated for a few minutes at the gate, where the children who lived outside the town were getting into their parents' cars. He waited until the noise in Castle Street died away before he set out for Cathedral Close where his grandmother lived.

The Castle Street boys would have gone home now—that gang of toughs who sometimes stood at the corner to jeer at him, because he came from the "Mollycoddle School", as they called it.

One afternoon they had knocked him down, and though he had not been really hurt, Gran was worried when he came home with his clothes dirty. Paul's parents had died when he was a baby, and since then he had lived

"I've got some news for you"

with Gran whom he loved more than anyone in the world.

She was waiting for him in the little sitting-room, where each piece of furniture shone like a mirror, and where nothing was ever out of place. One glance at her face showed him that something was wrong, though he knew he was as clean and tidy as she liked him to be, in spite of having run the last bit of the way so as not to be late.

"What is it, Gran? Is your cough bad again?" he asked anxiously.

"No, darling; it's no worse than usual. It's just—I've got some news for you. Sit down and have your tea, and I'll tell you about it."

Tea was the same as usual; very thin slices of bread and butter cut from one of the loaves specially baked for Gran, as she thought factory bread unwholesome; jelly in a glass jar, home-made sponge-cake, and a boiled egg for Paul in a pretty china egg-cup. Paul obediently started on his egg and listened to Gran's gentle voice telling him that the doctor wanted her to go to Switzerland for a few weeks, because of her cough.

"*Switzerland!* Oh, Gran, can I come too?" he burst out.

Her reproving look reminded him that she thought it rude to begin talking directly the other person had finished a sentence.

"You must wait until you are quite sure that the other people have no more to say," she had told him. Paul sometimes thought that, if everybody kept this rule, no one would ever say anything at all; but arguing was forbidden, and anyway Gran must know best.

"I have arranged for you to stay with your father's sister, Catherine Martin," she said now. "You'll be able to go to school with your three cousins. They live on a farm, and there are ponies to ride. You'll enjoy that, darling," she added, seeing that Paul looked doubtful. He had never seen the Martins, though his Aunt Cathy always sent him a present at Christmas.

"How old are they?" he asked, after pausing politely.

Gran guessed that he was not referring to the ponies. "I know there's a boy just your age," she murmured, as she picked up a letter and put on her spectacles.

" 'Margaret is nearly eleven,' " she read aloud. " 'Stephen is nine and Sally eight. I hope Paul will be happy at Ash Farm. We are all looking forward to having him here.' " Gran folded the letter and put it in the envelope. "I'm glad there'll be a boy for you to play with," she remarked. "And it will be good for Stephen to have you there. I expect he's rather girlish, coming between two sisters."

"How long do I have to stay there?" Paul asked shakily.

"Only till the end of the Easter holidays. I'll be back before the summer term starts," she said cheerfully. "The time will pass very quickly, and just think what a lot you'll have to tell me!"

Ash Farm

A FORTNIGHT later Paul was sitting in the front seat of a very old car, nearing the end of a three-hour journey. His Uncle Dick, who was driving, switched on the sidelights of the car. "It'll be nearly dark by the time we get home," he said. "I expect you'll be glad of your tea." The thought of tea was cheering, but Paul's sinking feeling was not entirely caused by hunger. He still had to meet Aunt Cathy and the three strange cousins. The road ran beside a very high stone wall, which Uncle Dick said enclosed the garden and grounds of a big house called Westfield, which had once belonged to his family.

"My father sold it to Miss Deborah Wynne,

the present owner," he told Paul. "He kept the home farm, which is where we live now."

The car slowed down, then turned into a

The car slowed down, then turned into a narrow lane

narrow lane, at the end of which was a low stone house. Uncle Dick sounded the horn several times as he drove round the house into a farmyard. He got out of the car and came round to open the door for Paul. There was an outburst of joyful barking as two large dogs hurled themselves on their master, nearly knocking Paul over, while a small terrier yapped around his ankles; but there was no sign of a human being. "I wonder where they've all got to," muttered Uncle Dick. "The place seems to be deserted." Then a man dressed in dungarees ran across the yard.

"The ponies are out again," he shouted. "Miss Midge rode off on the chestnut mare to try and round them up, and the two youngsters ran after her. I've got Caradoc saddled ready for you."

"Right! Bring him out for me, Jack, and I'll be off at once." Uncle Dick took the suitcase from the car and handed it to Paul.

"I'm sorry," he said. "I'll have to go after those wretched ponies. Come in this way, and your aunt will give you some tea. Cathy!" he called, opening a door which led straight into the kitchen. The light was on, and there were plates and cups on the table as if someone had started to get tea ready. "I expect she'll be here in a minute or two," Uncle Dick said, when he had called again and received no answer. "Sit down and make yourself at home. I wish I didn't have to leave you, but the dogs will keep you company." He hurried out to the yard where Jack was holding the bridle of a big grey horse. Paul went to the window, through which a beam of light fell on his uncle as he mounted and rode out of the yard. Then Paul heard him cantering along the road.

The three dogs whined and scratched at the door, longing to follow their master. Then they gave up in despair, and sniffed at Paul suspiciously. He didn't much like being shut in alone with them, but thought he had better not let them out. He wished with all his heart that he could be at home, having tea in Gran's pretty sitting-room. Nervously eyeing the dogs, he moved over to a chair and sat down. The biggest dog came and laid his head on Paul's knee, and when Paul stroked him, the little terrier jumped on his lap and licked his face.

Suddenly all three dogs rushed to the door, which opened to admit a person who Paul at first thought was a young girl.

Like Jack, she wore dungarees, and she had very short brown hair, a round rosy face, and laughing brown eyes.

"You poor dear boy! What a shame to leave you all alone your first evening," she exclaimed. She threw her arms round Paul and kissed him, and he realized, with surprise, that this must be his Aunt Cathy. She quickly filled a kettle and put it on the old-fashioned cooking stove, set a sliced loaf and a slab of cheese on the table, then opened a packet of chocolate biscuits and tipped them on to a plate.

"I never heard you arrive," she explained, as she measured tea into a big brown teapot. "I knew Dick would be late getting home, so I fed the pigs for him, and Jack and I did the milking together. I suppose Dick's gone to help the children round up the ponies?" She broke off and went to the window. "I thought I heard them," she murmured. "Midge insisted on taking Polly, and I'm not sure that she can manage her." Paul had imagined that his aunt's anxiety was for Midge's safety, and it was not till later that

B

he understood that she was far more worried about her mare.

Just as the kettle boiled, there was a clatter of hooves in the yard as Uncle Dick rode in on Caradoc, followed by a girl mounted on a beautiful chestnut mare and leading a pony by a halter. They dismounted, then Midge led the pony into the stable while her father held both horses. Above the deafening noise made by the barking of dogs and the stamping hooves, Aunt Cathy could be heard shouting to Midge that Polly must be led about to cool off. It added to the confusion when a boy and girl ran panting into the yard, each leading a shaggy Welsh pony.

Uncle Dick, who was unsaddling Caradoc, said something to the boy, who surrendered his pony to the younger girl and ran towards the house. As he burst into the kitchen, Paul remembered Gran's warning that his cousin Stephen might be "rather girlish". Stephen's face, hands, and clothes were plastered with mud; there was even mud on his untidy rust-coloured hair. He grinned cheerfully at Paul and said, "Hullo!", then started to tell his mother about the chase after the ponies, but she cut him short.

"Go and clean yourself up, then come and have tea," she commanded. "We won't wait for you, as Paul must be starving!"

"Good-o!" replied Stephen, and he crashed out of the room, to reappear in a suspiciously short time having scraped the worst off his face and hands. Aunt Cathy had poured out the tea and was rapidly spreading butter over the slices of bread. Stephen pushed the cheese towards Paul. "Help yourself," he invited. "If you're half as hungry as I am, we'll need another loaf."

Soon afterwards the girls came in, explaining that the ponies and horses were still sweating and would have to be fed and watered after tea. "This is Midge, and that's Sally," Aunt Cathy told Paul. They both said "Hullo" in a friendly way, and Midge added that she was sorry they hadn't been there when he arrived.

Then all three children started talking at once, while they ate slice after slice of bread and cheese, and Paul glanced shyly from one to the other. Both the girls looked like boys, with their short hair and riding-breeches. Sally had her mother's colouring, but Midge was dark and seemed rather quieter than the others. Though as eager as they were to tell of their adventures, she saw to it that Paul had enough to eat and refilled his cup without being asked.

"But *how* did the ponies get loose?" asked their mother, when she could get a word in.

"The gate was open!" shouted Sally. "Steve is *sure* he latched it this morning, so someone must have let them out on purpose."

"It's the third time!" put in Steve. "We've got to find out who it is."

"We must go and feed the poor things now," Midge said, when they had finished tea. But Aunt Cathy told Steve to take Paul upstairs first.

"He hasn't seen his room yet, and he'll want to unpack," she said.

"You're to share with me. Come on, and I'll show you," Steve said, leading the way. Carrying his suitcase, Paul followed him up a narrow staircase, and into the untidiest room he had ever seen.

"Can you manage all right, if I go and help Dad and the girls?" asked Steve. "Just shove my things out of the way, if you want more room." He thundered down the stairs, and Paul slowly unpacked the clothes which Gran had folded so beautifully. He had known it would take time to get used to a strange place, but this house and family were like nothing he's ever imagined. Judging by Gran's standards, the Martins were not very polite, and he decided that Steve must be a very naughty boy to leave his clothes and other belongings lying all over the place. He thought it rather hard that he should be made to sleep in such an untidy room. It didn't occur to him that Steve was being extremely nice about having to share his very own room which was small enough to begin with, and was now uncomfortably crowded by the addition of a second bed.

Paul's Bible was at the bottom of the case, and as he laid it on the bed he remembered Gran's making him promise not to forget his daily prayers and reading. It seemed such a long time ago that she had said that, and he felt so far away, that it was difficult not to cry. And then, just at the right moment, Aunt Cathy entered, saying that they'd had tea so late, she had only just realized it was long past everyone's bedtime. "Why don't you undress and get to bed now?" she suggested. "It's been a long day for you, and though it's Saturday and there's no school, Steve may wake you when he goes out to see to all the animals." She pretended not to notice that Paul was trying to push a tear back into the corner of his eye.

When he had said his prayers and got into bed, she picked up his Bible and asked if he followed a special system for his daily reading. He showed her the leaflet which told him what to read each day, and she asked if he would like her first to read him a story about a boy who had to leave his home for the first time. Then, in the 28th chapter of Genesis, she read about Jacob, who felt very sad and lonely as he lay on the ground with stones for his pillow. But God sent him a dream of angels, and when Jacob woke he said: "Surely the Lord is in this place, and I knew it not."

As Aunt Cathy handed the Bible to Paul, she said: "Never forget that God is always with you, even when you are far from home." Then she tucked him up and kissed him, and said she would tell Steve to undress quietly so as not to wake him.

Paul didn't feel like talking, so pretended to be asleep, peeping through half-closed eyes when Steve tiptoed in, carrying his clothes as he had undressed in the bathroom. He accidentally dropped one of his shoes, then tripped over it, and altogether made far more noise than if he had undressed in the ordinary way.

3

A Stranger in the Orchard

THE sun had not yet risen when Paul woke to find his cousin up and dressed. "It's only half past six!" he protested sleepily, after consulting the new wristwatch which had been a parting present from Gran.

"We have to be out earlier than this on school mornings," Steve replied cheerfully. "There are the ponies to feed and water, and the rabbits and guinea-pigs and my hamster; and on Saturdays I help Dad and Jack with the farm animals. But you needn't get up yet, if you don't want to." He pulled his tumbled bedclothes over the bed and made a clumsy attempt to tuck in the sides. Then he knelt down and closed his eyes; but he was up again in a minute or two, so he couldn't have done much praying. Paul remembered that the same thing had happened on the evening before, and that Steve hadn't read his Bible at all.

Paul lay down again, but he no longer felt sleepy. He heard voices and footsteps and the clanking of buckets in the yard outside, while crockery rattled in the kitchen below his room. Soon he got up and looked out of the window. Uncle Dick was crossing the yard, carrying a bucket in each hand, and in a paddock beyond the yard the three ponies crowded round Steve while he hung nets of hay on the wooden rails. Paul noticed how carefully Steve secured the gate when he left the paddock, using both hands to push the stiff iron latch into place.

Paul had difficulty in following the lively discussion at the breakfast table, as his cousins all talked at once, interrupting each other in a way Gran would never have allowed. But he understood that they were going to ride, and were arguing about which pony should be lent to Paul.

"Have you done much riding?" Uncle Dick asked him.

"Oh yes! I've been going to the riding-school every week," Paul replied.

His uncle looked thoughtful. "You'd better lend him Taffy to start with," he told Sally. "You and Steve must take turns riding Bryn. Riding-school ponies are worked very hard, while these don't get much exercise during term," he explained to Paul. "But all these children learnt to ride on Taffy, and he's very quiet."

Paul felt rather put out by the suggestion that he couldn't manage any but the quietest pony, and he didn't notice the good natured way in which Sally agreed to surrender her own property.

But when, later, he accompanied Midge and Steve as they rode over to a neighbouring farm with a message, he found that it was as much as he could do to manage Taffy. Midge's pony, Heather, danced about the yard before they started, and Bryn did her best to buck Steve off. All three ponies were fresh, but they quietened down after a canter

Paul began to enjoy his ride

up a hill near the house, and then Paul began
to enjoy his ride.

When they turned the ponies out in the
paddock, Midge showed Paul how to fasten
the gate. "It's quite awkward if you don't

know the trick of it," she said. "And if it's not done the right way, the cunning little brutes have found a way of pushing it open!"

She had to do her usual Saturday job of cleaning out the hen-houses, but Paul never thought of helping her. He hung about feeling bored, till Steve came and offered to show him round the farm. They visited the pigs and a new-born calf, then went to look at a brood of ducklings in the orchard. At the far end of the orchard was a high wall with barbed wire along the top. Paul recognized it as a continuation of the wall he had seen from the road, which enclosed Westfield, Uncle Dick's old home.

"Do you ever go there?" he asked.

Steve chuckled. "We used to; but Miss Wynne won't have us there now, because of Jemima." Paul thought "Jemima" must be a fierce dog, till Steve explained that it was their nickname for Miss Wynne's nephew James. "He's about our age, but he's more like a girl than a boy . . . always swanking about his best clothes."

"He doesn't sound very like *these* girls,"

laughed Paul, glancing at Midge who was raking the litter out of a hen-house.

"Well, no, Midge and Sally are different," Steve agreed. "But just you wait till you see Jemima. He's not allowed to come here, for fear he should learn our rough ways!"

During the rest of the day, Paul kept thinking about the boy next door. He believed he might get on better with James than with his cousins, who seemed always to be working, and the dirtier the job the more they appeared to enjoy it.

"Can't you find anything to do?" Aunt Cathy asked after tea, when she found Paul gazing out of the play-room window while the rest of the family were feeding and watering the animals.

This room had a bare wooden floor, and there were plenty of games stacked against the walls, but they were not the sort you could play alone. "Would you like to come and help me wash the eggs?" she suggested, but Paul said he felt like reading, and went upstairs to fetch one of the books he had brought with him.

At bed-time he was surprised to find Steve actually reading a Bible. Looking over his shoulder, Paul noticed that his cousin was using a leaflet like his own. "But you're reading the Wednesday portion," he pointed out. "It's Saturday today."

"I've some catching up to do," Steve told him cheerfully. "We're supposed to read every day, and Mum asks questions about it on Sunday. But I usually forget, and have to swot it all up on Saturday night."

Paul felt very superior as he read his daily portion, then knelt and went through the form of prayer Gran had taught him. He was already in bed when Steve closed his Bible with a sigh of relief.

"You'd find it easier to read a bit every day, like I do," Paul said primly.

"Sez you!" Steve retorted good-humouredly. "But shut up now, as I've got something special to say tonight." He dropped to his knees, and as Paul watched his lips moving, he felt that he would never understand this family. Steve had spoken as naturally as if he had decided to have a chat with a friend.

Paul sat up in bed, wondering why he'd woken so early. It was only twenty minutes to six, and Steve was still asleep. A second whinny from the ponies' paddock reminded him that this was the sound which had woken him. He jumped out of bed and ran to the window, just in time to see a stranger leaving the paddock—a slim, dark-haired boy wearing a ragged sweater and muddy jeans. Paul hid behind the curtain as the boy glanced up at the house. He had difficulty in fastening the gate, and even from that distance, Paul could see that he hadn't done it properly. The boy wore gym-shoes and his feet made no sound as he ran lightly down the lane. He had hardly turned the corner when Taffy began to work his nose up and down on the latch, while Heather leant sideways against the gate.

"Steve!" cried Paul, but Steve only grunted and turned over on his side. Paul thrust his bare feet into his shoes and, putting a coat over his pyjamas, ran downstairs. The kitchen door was bolted on the inside. Paul clenched his teeth and pushed with all his might, pinching his fingers as the bolt shot back. Then, at last, he was out in the cold air, racing across the yard. He was only just in time; in another moment, the gate would have swung open. Even now, he was not sure that he could fasten it by himself.

"Hullo! What's up?" It was Uncle Dick, fully dressed, striding across the yard.

"The ponies! The gate . . . there was a boy . . . he didn't fasten the gate properly." Paul was so breathless with relief that at first he was quite unable to explain what had happened. His uncle took him into the kitchen and made tea for them both, and while they drank it, Paul described what he had seen.

"Good man! So you dealt with it all on your own. I suppose that lazy young Steve is still asleep!"

"I didn't manage the gate by myself," Paul said; and he added truthfully—"I wouldn't have gone out alone if I'd been able to wake Steve." But his uncle's praise made him feel warm and happy. He had been rather out of things, but now he felt he really belonged here.

4

The Boy Next Door

ALL through breakfast the family discussed Paul's discovery, and wondered who the ragged boy could be.

"P'r'aps he's a gipsy!" suggested Sally, her brown eyes dancing with excitement. Uncle Dick said that he hadn't heard of any gipsy camp in the neighbourhood, and that in any case the boy hadn't tried to steal the ponies.

"He might have been sent on ahead to spy out the land for the others. *I* think we should keep watch all night," Steve declared.

"Paul says the boy *tried* to shut the gate. So this does away with the idea that someone lets them out on purpose," put in Midge.

Paul had dressed in his Sunday suit, but all the others were in working clothes as the

animals must be cared for on Sundays as well
as on weekdays. Then there was a rush to get
changed, and Steve nearly made them late
for church by saying that he didn't want to go,
as someone ought to stay and guard the
ponies.

"This happens most Sundays! If it isn't
one excuse, it's another," Midge told Paul,
who was looking shocked and disapproving,
though he had often wished he could miss
church but had never said so out loud. They
got there just in time; and as they crowded
into a pew, Steve nudged Paul.

"That's Jemima!" he whispered, directing
Paul's attention to a boy who sat with a tall
grey-haired lady on the other side of the aisle.
Paul could understand why Miss Wynne had
decided that the young Martins were not
suitable companions for James.

He wore a very smart grey-flannel suit
with a spotless white shirt, and his curly hair
was as smooth as brushing could make it.
He never once fidgeted or stared at other
people, and it was impossible to imagine him
getting dirty or untidy. Paul wished he could

get to know him, but didn't see how it was to be managed. However, after church Miss Wynne waylaid Aunt Cathy and stood talking

James must be the twin brother of the ragged urchin

to her, while the rest of the Ash Farm party walked on. Then Aunt Cathy called Paul back and introduced him to Miss Wynne, who said she had met his grandmother, and that she would like him to come to tea with James that afternoon.

"Come here, James, and shake hands with Paul," she commanded, and Paul gave a start of surprise when he found himself face to face with the other boy. If he had not known it was impossible, he would have said that James must be the twin brother of the ragged urchin who had visited the paddock that morning.

All through lunch Paul's cousins teased him about the invitation. "Poor you! Fancy having to go to tea with Jemima!" exclaimed Sally.

"You'd better lend Paul a skirt, Midge," Steve suggested. "Don't forget to take your sewing, Paul, and one of Sally's dolls."

"Don't pay any attention to them, Paul," advised Aunt Cathy. "I didn't like to refuse for you, as I think that poor boy is very lonely." She explained that James's parents had gone abroad for a year, and that his Aunt Deborah Wynne was secretary to a big hospital in the county town, and spent all her free time at committee meetings. She drove

James to a little school in the town on her way to the hospital, and fetched him from there on her way home.

"A sissy kind of private school," added Steve. "He's not allowed to go to our school in the village here."

"It's no life for a boy," muttered Uncle Dick. "His parents should never have sent him to Westfield."

"You must try and cheer him up," Aunt Cathy told Paul. "Now, be quick all of you, because it's time for Bible Questions."

Steve groaned, and said he'd forgotten every word he'd read, but Paul's face lit up. Here, at last, was something he could do better than the Martins! However, he soon found that he was mistaken. Carefully as he had studied the week's daily readings, he was not prepared for the sort of questions asked by Aunt Cathy.

She seemed to expect them to understand the meaning of the stories and parables, and how they ought to follow the teaching of Jesus in their daily lives. Paul was the best at remembering the actual words, but as he'd never thought of connecting the parables with himself, he was unable to answer any of the questions. But when Aunt Cathy asked if there was anything which had puzzled them in the readings, he was the first to speak.

"It seems so unfair," he said. "When the Pharisee and the Publican went into the temple to pray, *why* should God have been pleased with the Publican who was a sinner, and not pleased with the Pharisee who had done everything right?"

"Please, Mummy, may I say?" pleaded Sally. But her mother said she would like Midge to explain, perhaps because she wanted Paul to understand.

"The Publican knew he was a sinner," Midge said shyly. "And he repented and asked God to have mercy on him."

"And why wasn't God pleased with the Pharisee?" prompted her mother.

"Because he was stuck up and conceited," said Steve.

"*No*, Steve! What was really wrong was that he thought he didn't need to be forgiven," corrected Sally.

"But he'd done all those good things, so he *didn't* need forgiveness," argued Paul. "Anyway, not so much as the Publican did."

He thought Aunt Cathy was changing the subject when she asked her children if, when they went to the big Horse Show, they'd had enough money to pay the entrance fee.

"No, Dad had to pay for us all," Midge remembered. "I'd been saving up my pocket money, but it wasn't enough."

"So without Dad you'd have been turned away from the gate, just the same as Steve and Sally who hadn't any money at all," said her mother. "You see, Paul, not one of us is good enough to enter God's kingdom; we are all equally in need of the forgiveness Christ paid for when He died on the cross."

"Do you think Paul understood?" she asked Midge privately, when Paul had gone to Westfield.

"I'm not sure," replied Midge. "He—he—it sounds a horrid thing to say, but he's rather like the Pharisee, really." Neither of them noticed that Sally was listening, till she suddenly chipped in.

"Paul's awfully religious and goody-goody, but Steve's a much nicer person, though he says he can't be bothered."

"It's not that he can't be bothered, it's just that he wants to decide things for himself, instead of asking Christ to rule his life," said Midge. "And it's been worse since Paul came, because Steve says all that praying and Bible-reading doesn't stop Paul from being frightfully selfish and lazy."

"It's so easy to see when a person doesn't belong to Christ," sighed Mrs. Martin. "It ought to work the other way too, don't you think?"

Midge turned red, and Sally said: "You mean we ought to *show* that Christ has come into our lives? But how? We can't even see Him ourselves."

"You can't see the sun from where you're sitting," her mother pointed out. "But you know it's shining, because this room is full of warmth and light. If Paul and Steve could see the love of God shining in our lives, in all we say and do, I'm sure they'd want to belong to Him too."

5

Jimmy's Secret

MEANWHILE, Paul was sitting at Miss Wynne's tea-table which reminded him of his grandmother's. It ought to have made him feel at home, and he was surprised to find himself missing the noisy cheerful meals at Ash Farm. James hardly spoke at all, though he was very polite about handing things. They were having tea early, as Miss Wynne. had to go and visit a friend afterwards. "You may show Paul round the garden," she told James before she left. "But don't get your clothes dirty, and come indoors before it gets cold." She explained to Paul that having a boy to stay was a great responsibility when she had to be away so often, so she had made a set of very strict rules which James had to obey.

As soon as she had driven off in her little car, James turned to Paul. "You *are* lucky to be staying with the Martins!" he blurted out. "I wish I could go back there with you."

"I—I didn't know you—you liked them," stammered Paul.

"I've never spoken to them," James said sadly. "But I often watch them from my look-out post." He pointed to the high branch of a chestnut tree which grew near the dividing wall.

"How do you get up there without messing up your clothes?" Paul wanted to know.

"I'll show you!" James led the way to a small shed behind the house. From behind a stack of wooden boxes he produced a bundle consisting of a torn jersey, a pair of jeans, and some grubby gym-shoes. Pulling off his Sunday clothes he quickly dressed himself in the shabby outfit, and Paul gave a gasp of surprise.

"So it was *you* I saw with the ponies this morning!" he exclaimed.

He quickly dressed himself in the shabby outfit

James nodded. "I take apple-cores, and any tit-bits I can save for them. I had a pony at home, so I know what they like to eat." It was a great shock to him to learn that his unsuccessful attempts to fasten the gate had resulted in the ponies escaping, and he begged Paul to tell the Martins how dreadfully sorry he was. He asked so many eager questions about the ponies and their owners, and spoke so wistfully, that Paul began to feel he was extremely lucky to be living with such exciting people.

"What a pity you can't come and join us," he said.

"I'm going to, one day," James said mysteriously. "If you'll promise not to tell, I'll let you into a secret."

Paul followed him through a dense shrubbery till they reached the foot of the wall. Beneath a covering of dead leaves was an old tin tray. James lifted it, and exposed a large, deep hole in the ground. "Aunt Deborah's forbidden me to go through the gate without permission, when she's not at home, but she didn't say anything about going underground," he laughed, and wriggled into the hole till nothing could be seen but the soles of his shoes.

"It's a secret tunnel," he panted when he had backed out. He was caked with damp earth; Paul had never seen even Steve look like this. "I haven't got under the wall yet; the foundations go down so deep," continued James. "But one day I shall get through to the other side. That is, if you think your cousins won't mind?" he added.

"I should think they'll be frightfully pleased, when—when they know what you're really like," replied Paul. "But, James— can't I tell Steve about the tunnel? And perhaps Midge and Sally too? I'm sure they won't give away the secret."

"I hate being called James. I'm always called Jimmy, at home. Yes, I'd like you to tell them. And if they think it's a good idea, they might start tunnelling from the other side."

Jimmy climbed nimbly up the chestnut tree, and Paul followed—rather clumsily as he wasn't used to climbing. From the look-out post they marked a spot in the Martins' orchard which was exactly opposite Jimmy's tunnel.

It took Jimmy a long time to get the dirt

Jimmy climbed nimbly up the chestnut tree

off his face and hands; but when Miss Wynne returned, she found two clean and tidily-dressed boys.

Paul had been dreading the new school, but it wasn't as bad as he'd expected. Being

Steve's cousin, he escaped the ragging he would otherwise have received for being a duffer at games and far ahead of the others in class. When they were in the playground, Steve was never far from his side, and Paul noticed this and was grateful. He was, in fact, discovering a great many things he had missed during his first days at Ash Farm. Jimmy's words had opened his eyes, and he had begun to notice that Midge was always careful not to hurt other people's feelings, and that Sally was very good-tempered as well as being very plucky when she hurt herself. Steve was sometimes impatient, but Paul now knew that his rough manner was mostly a pretence to conceal his kind and generous nature.

The two boys were nearly always together now, because Paul helped Steve with the animals after tea. By dividing the jobs between them, they finished in half the time, and were able to work at their end of the secret passage while there was still enough light to see what they were doing, for the Martin children had been thrilled by Paul's

He grinned cheerfully at Paul

account of Jimmy—who was no longer called Jemima—and they looked forward to secret meetings underground.

On the Martins' side, the tunnel was progressing fast; Steve and Paul took turns to dig, while the others cleared the earth out of the way. Miss Wynne had given Paul an open invitation to come to her garden whenever he liked, and he was able to report on Jimmy's progress. This was slower than theirs, since nobody thought of asking how they spent their spare time, while Jimmy could only change into his working clothes when his Aunt Deborah was out.

One evening Steve wriggled backwards out of the hole and declared that he could hear Jimmy burrowing on the other side. "I reckon we'll break through tomorrow!" he said.

It was now quite dark, and Paul was secretly glad to down tools and go indoors. He wished he was like Steve, who never seemed to get tired however hard he worked. The more he admired his cousin, the more

D

dissatisfied he felt with himself. "I've been just like that Pharisee," he thought. "Being good on the outside, but really rather horrid underneath." He felt hot as he remembered the times he'd shirked helping with the daily jobs; how he had been selfish with his possessions, and found fault with Steve, who was ten times nicer than he could ever be.

"I don't know how you boys manage to get into such a filthy state every day," exclaimed Aunt Cathy. "However, a hot bath will soon put that right. Don't forget to clean the bath when you've finished."

Paul wished he could get rid of all his horridness as easily as he scrubbed away the earth. "What did the Publican mean when he asked God to have mercy?" he demanded abruptly.

"What Publican?" spluttered Steve, who had just plunged his soapy head under water.

"*You* know, the one who went into the temple when the Pharisee was there. He said: 'be merciful to me a sinner.' Was he asking God to forgive him?"

"I suppose so," muttered Steve. He got out of the bath and rubbed himself vigorously. "And to give him a fresh start . . . and all that sort of thing. I say! Hurry up and get out, or the water will be cold."

"I'd like a new start," Paul said wistfully, when they were in their bedroom. "I hate being me. I wish I was like you."

Steve turned crimson. "That wouldn't do you any good," he snapped. "You see, I don't want to do it."

"Do what?"

"I don't want to ask Christ to come in and take over my life," mumbled Steve. "I reckon I get on all right by myself."

"But—I thought you knew Him quite well," Paul protested. "You said you'd told Him how worried you were about the ponies getting loose . . . and the very next day we found that Jimmy had done it by accident." Steve didn't answer, and he looked so cross that Paul said no more. He was thinking that it was all very well for a splendid person like Steve to manage alone; but his own life was in such a dreadful muddle, he wouldn't wait another moment before asking Jesus Christ to come and put it straight, and never leave him again.

Steve didn't pray at all that night. He missed having his private talk with God, but it didn't seem fair to claim Him as a friend when he had refused to be a disciple.

Two days later, Paul heard a muffled shout from Steve who was down in the tunnel. This was his signal to crawl in till he could grasp Steve's feet and pull him out.

"We're *through*!" grasped Steve, when he had spat out a mouthful of earth. "I must have been right under the wall. I could hear Jim scraping away, and it sounded so close I bored a hole with the trowel and he caught hold of my hand!"

"Good-O!" said Paul, who had caught that expression from Steve. Steve thrust the trowel into his hand. "You'd better take this. It's only a tiny hole, and the earth keeps falling in and blocking it. There's a lot of work to be done before we can crawl through."

"What *are* you doing!" Neither of the boys

had heard Mr. Martin coming across the grass, but now they swung round and faced him.

"It's our secret passage, Dad, and we've just got to Jimmy's side!" replied Steve. "He'll soon be able to crawl through! We didn't want anyone to know, but you won't tell Miss Wynne, will you?"

"Didn't she forbid James to come here?" demanded his father sternly.

"She told him not to go through the gate while she was out. She said nothing about going underground," argued Paul.

Mr. Martin looked the boys up and down. The earth was sticky after a heavy rain, and they looked as if they'd been carved out of chocolate. Then he glanced at the gaping hole, and back again at the boys. His face twitched in such a queer way that Paul thought he must be very angry, but he spoke gently.

"I'm sure neither of you meant to cheat, and I don't suppose James did, either. To come here openly would be disobedient and very wrong, but it would have been more honest than this. You've been helping him to be deceitful."

"We never thought of that," Steve admitted.

"That's the trouble. You don't stop to think. Besides, this secret passage is thoroughly dangerous. The damp ground could fall in at any time. How would you like to be buried under there?"

The boys hadn't thought of that either, and the idea was not a pleasant one. "This hole must be filled in at once," Mr. Martin continued. "You'd better start now, Steve, and you, Paul, cut along to James and tell him to do the same."

Paul ran off, feeling dreadfully ashamed of himself. He was one of Christ's disciples now, but how badly he had let Him down!

Steve felt very cross as he shovelled back the earth which had taken so long to dig out. He saw now that his father was right and that the tunnel plan had been a sort of cheating, but it was nonsense to say it was dangerous. For the hundredth time he wished that grown-up people would leave him alone to run things his own way. He was well able to look after himself, without interference from anyone else.

His gloomy thoughts were interrupted by a shout from the other side of the wall. "Come here, Steve! *Quick! Hurry!*"

Still holding the spade, Steve raced across the orchard, down the lane and along the road to the Westfield gate. He wasn't supposed to go in, but Paul had sounded desperate, as if something terrible had happened. Steve had a wild idea that Miss Wynne had caught them filling in the hole; but when he burst through the shrubbery he saw that Miss Wynne wasn't there and neither was Jimmy, and instead of replacing the earth in the tunnel, Paul was digging it out as fast as he could. "He's in there, and I can't get at him," he sobbed. "The roof of the tunnel fell in . . . and Jimmy's trapped."

Steve didn't waste time in talking, but began to dig feverishly.

"Careful with that spade, we must be near him now," Paul warned him. "He called out

—just as I got here. Said he was stuck . . . couldn't get back. Then—a lot more earth fell on top of him——" He broke off, but Steve saw that his lips were moving.

"He's praying," thought Steve. "I want to pray, too, but will God hear me? I don't deserve to be heard—I've no right to ask— I'm too far away." Then he remembered that no one, of himself, deserves God's mercy; that it is only through Jesus Christ that we can approach God. Was it too late to make a new start, now, when he was in such dreadful trouble?

Steve had always grumbled when he was made to learn verses from the Bible, but now he thought of Jonah who had called to God when he was in the depths of the sea, inside the great fish.

"I cried by reason of my affliction unto the Lord, and he heard me." And Peter had been actually sinking in the waves when he cried: "Lord, save me!"

"Lord, save me," whispered Steve. "I'm sorry I've left it so late, but please hear me and—have mercy."

"Stop! Look out!" yelled Paul. He dropped the spade and, kneeling down, started to scrape away the loose earth with his hands.

They worked desperately

Still praying silently, Steve followed his example. They had uncovered Jimmy's feet, and they now worked desperately to remove the rest of the earth from his unconscious form. Neither dared say what was in his mind—that they were too late, that Jimmy must be dead. They were too engrossed to hear Miss Wynne's car, but suddenly she was kneeling beside them, gently running her hands over Jimmy, bending down to listen.

"He's breathing," she said quietly. "Help me to carry him indoors," she told Steve. "And you, Paul, ring up the doctor and ask him to come at once. You know where the telephone is, and his number is on a card beside it."

Paul was very shy of using the telephone, but he managed to dial the number and was in time to catch the doctor at his surgery. He promised to be at Westfield in a few minutes.

While Paul was telephoning, Jimmy had been laid on the drawing-room sofa. As soon as he recovered consciousness he was sick, choking up the earth he had swallowed.

"How could it have happened?" Miss Wynne was saying when Paul entered the room. "I didn't know that pit was there. If it hadn't been for you two boys . . . how can I ever thank you?"

"But it's all our fault!" exclaimed Steve. "Jim had started making an underground passage to get to us, and we were tunnelling on the other side."

He and Paul had always thought Jimmy's aunt was a stiff, unbending sort of person, and they were startled to see the tears run down her face. "If I had known! If only I'd known!" she kept saying. "He must have been so lonely . . . and I never knew!"

"But he's had Paul," Steve said consolingly. Like all his family, he couldn't bear anyone to be unhappy.

"He only likes me because I'm Steve's cousin," Paul pointed out. "You see, he'd always wanted to make friends with the Martins."

CHAPTER

6

Aunt Deborah Changes her Mind

STEVE'S parents had guessed something
was wrong, and they arrived at the same
time as the doctor. Mr. Martin told the boys
to go home and carry on with the farm work,
while he waited to see if he could be of any
use. When he returned to the farm, he was
able to report that there was nothing seriously
wrong with Jimmy, except for a cracked rib.
He told the boys he would say nothing more
about the tunnelling. "I think you see, now,
how dangerous it is," he said. "And Miss
Wynne made me promise not to scold you!"

A few days later, Miss Wynne called at
Ash Farm. She found Midge in the kitchen,
feeding a lamb with a baby's bottle, while
Sally had let the hamster out of its hutch and

it was running about the room. Sally offered
to fetch her mother who was shutting up the
hens, and Midge pulled forward a chair for
the visitor, who said she had really come to
see Paul and Steve. They had been feeding
the ponies, but came running when Sally
called them.

"Poor James has to stay in bed for a week,"
Miss Wynne told them. "It's very dull for
him, and I'd be grateful if you'd both come
and see him whenever you can spare the
time."

"Good-O," said Steve. "Shall we come
now?" But Paul suggested that they should
first clean themselves up.

"I think James would rather see you just
as you are," said their visitor.

So the boys walked back with her, and she
saw Jimmy's face break into a broad smile
when his friends entered the room.

When she had gone, Jimmy said: "Do stay
as long as you can. But you mustn't say
anything funny, as it hurts me to laugh!"

"Holidays start tomorrow," Paul told him.
"We can come here whenever you like."

"After we've finished the jobs at home," Steve reminded him.

"Aunt Deborah says I may come and help you, when I'm about again," Jimmy said shyly. "That is, if you won't mind."

"That'll be smashing," chorused the others, but Paul added: "We get awfully grubby, you know."

"Aunt Deborah doesn't mind that now," Jimmy assured them. "She thinks you're a splendid family, and she wants me to be at Ash Farm as often as you'll have me."

"Good-O!" said Steve.